BASED ON THE
HIT MOVIE!

Annie

A TRUE FAMILY

ADAPTED BY CALLIOPE GLASS

**BASED ON THE SCREENPLAY
BY WILL GLUCK AND ALINE BROSH MCKENNA**

**BASED ON THE MUSICAL STAGE PLAY: BOOK BY THOMAS MEEHAN,
MUSIC BY CHARLES STROUSE, AND LYRICS BY MARTIN CHARNIN**

No part of this publication may be reproduced in whole or in part, stored in a retrieval system,
or transmitted in any form or by any means, electronic, mechanical, photocopying, recording, or otherwise,
without written permission of the publisher. For information regarding permission, write to Scholastic Inc.,
Attention: Permissions Department, 557 Broadway, New York, NY 10012.

ISBN 978-0-545-79752-8

Annie and related characters and elements: TM & © 2014 Tribune Content Agency, LLC.

Annie, the Movie © 2014 Columbia Pictures Industries, Inc. All Rights Reserved.

Published by Scholastic Inc. SCHOLASTIC and associated logos are trademarks and/or
registered trademarks of Scholastic Inc.

12 11 10 9 8 7 6 5 4 3 2 1   14 15 16 17 18 19/0

Printed in the U.S.A.   40

First printing, November 2014

SCHOLASTIC INC.

Annie Bennett was *not* an orphan.

She just didn't know who her parents were. They had left her outside a police station when she was a baby with a note:

Please take care of Annie.
We'll be back to get her soon. There's
half a locket with her and we have the
other half, so you'll know she's our girl.

Ever since then, Annie had lived in a foster home in New York City. But she knew she would find her true family someday.

Annie lived at the foster home with four other girls. They loved to hear her talk about her parents.

"We all have families somewhere," Annie told them.

Miss Hannigan ran the foster home. She was mean to the girls. She made them clean the house but never helped.

"The city's coming to inspect!" she yelled at them one morning. "You have to clean the whole place up!"

Miss Hannigan made the girls pretend to be happy for the inspector. "You! Read a book. And you! Braid her hair."

The girls did their best to look cheerful when the inspector arrived. "How's everyone doing?" he asked them.

"Living the dream," Annie replied.

   While Miss Hannigan was talking to the inspector, Annie snuck out of the house. Outside, some kids were chasing a stray dog.

   "Hey!" she yelled. "Leave it alone!"

Annie ran to stop them as fast as she could. She didn't look where she was going.

Bam! She ran right into someone. Annie fell backward into the busy street.

Screech! A van was coming toward her! It was going to hit her!

Suddenly, someone yanked Annie back onto the sidewalk.

"Sorry!" Annie said to the man who had saved her.

"Don't be sorry," he said. "Just be careful. Why are you running?"

"It gets me places quicker!" Annie said with a grin.

The man who saved Annie was named Will Stacks. He owned a cell phone company and was very rich. He was also running to be the mayor of New York City.

Saving a little girl from being hit by a car was good for his popularity.

"This is fantastic, Will!" Mr. Stacks's campaign manager, Guy, said. "Invite her to lunch. The press will eat it up."

Annie was excited to have lunch with Mr. Stacks. She understood what was going on. The more she and Mr. Stacks were seen together, the better it was for his campaign. And the more she could be out of the foster home!

"I bet if I moved in with you, you'd become president," Annie told him.

Guy clapped his hands. "That's not a bad idea!"

So Annie came to stay with Mr. Stacks just until his campaign was over.

"Whoa," Annie said. Mr. Stacks's house was *amazing*!

There was a tennis court and a swimming pool and a piano.

There was even a machine in the kitchen that made hot cocoa with fresh whipped cream.

But the best part was Annie's room. It had the biggest, softest bed Annie had ever slept in. She loved it right away.

The first thing Annie and Mr. Stacks did was go to Central Park together. They played soccer. Then they played on the swing set. Mr. Stacks carried Annie on his shoulders. Annie made sure the reporters saw her having fun.

Next, Mr. Stacks took Annie to a shelter to adopt a dog. Annie couldn't believe her eyes! There was the stray dog she had tried to save the other day.

"Hey, girl," Annie said to the dog. "We found each other!" She named the dog Sandy and promised to never leave her.

That night, Annie couldn't sleep. Mr. Stacks's house was very quiet, and she missed her foster sisters. She went into the kitchen. Mr. Stacks was there, working. He was always working.

"When do you have fun?" Annie asked.

"This is fun," Mr. Stacks said.

Annie thought Mr. Stacks must be pretty lonely.

Meanwhile, the press absolutely adored Annie. She was becoming a star! She went to a movie premiere with Mr. Stacks and his coworker, Grace. Everyone recognized her. Annie felt very special.

The movie premiere was for a kids' film. Mr. Stacks let Annie bring her foster sisters to see it! But he wanted to leave before the movie started.

"Can't you stay and see the movie?" Annie asked.

She thought Mr. Stacks could use some *real* fun in his life.
Mr. Stacks stayed for the movie . . . and he liked it!

Annie was glad. It was nice to see Mr. Stacks finally having a good time.

Because of Annie, Mr. Stacks was more popular than ever. He might even *win* the race for mayor of New York City!

He brought Annie with him to a big charity event. It was a lot of fun . . . until Guy told Annie to read a speech to everyone.

"No!" Annie said. She ran off the stage.

"What's wrong?" Mr. Stacks asked Annie.

"I can't read," Annie said. It was her biggest secret. "I'm good at hiding it so people will think I'm smart."

Mr. Stacks put an arm around Annie. "You *are* smart. And I promise we're going to teach you to read."

Meanwhile, Guy had a sneaky campaign idea. If Mr. Stacks found Annie's parents, he was certain to win the election!

But Guy didn't care about finding Annie's *real* parents. He just cared about making it look like they did.

Later that night, Mr. Stacks tucked Annie into bed. His life was so much more fun with her in it. He felt sad about sending her back to the foster home once his campaign was over.

If only . . .

If only he could adopt her and be her father.

But Mr. Stacks didn't get the chance to tell Annie how he felt. The next morning, Guy rushed into his office.

"We found Annie's parents!" he cried.

"You found my parents?" Annie asked. She couldn't believe it!

Mr. Stacks was happy for Annie, but he was also sad.

Guy brought Annie and Mr. Stacks to meet Annie's parents. Annie was very nervous.

"Annie!" her father cried when he saw her.

"My girl!" her mother said. She held out the other half of Annie's locket.

"Are we sure about this?" Mr. Stacks asked Guy. He had a bad feeling. Something about Annie's parents didn't seem quite right.

"Don't worry. This is going to win you the election," Guy insisted.

Soon, it was time for Annie to say good-bye to Mr. Stacks. She was happy she'd found her parents . . . but she was also sad to leave. She had grown to really like Mr. Stacks.

"I made you something," she said. She handed him a card she had drawn.

"Bye, Annie," Mr. Stacks said. He hugged her tightly.

As soon as they were in the car, Annie's parents stopped smiling at her. They stopped being nice to her. In fact, they stopped talking to her at all.

Something was very wrong.

"You're not my parents, are you?" Annie said. Suddenly, she was afraid.

Annie's "mom" and "dad" weren't her real parents at all. Guy had just hired them to pretend! All he cared about was making Mr. Stacks look like a hero. He didn't care about Annie.

Mr. Stacks figured out what was going on and was furious.

"She's just one girl," Guy told him.

"She's all *I* care about," Mr. Stacks said. He couldn't believe Guy had done this. It didn't matter if it cost him the election. He had to save Annie!

Meanwhile, Annie needed to escape. The car doors and windows were locked. But at a stoplight, some kids in the next car over saw her and snapped her picture.

That gave Annie an idea! She kept getting kids' attention so they would take her picture.

Mr. Stacks, Grace, and Annie's foster sisters saw the pictures start to pop up online. The kids were posting them to the Internet!

Quickly, Mr. Stacks used the cell phone pictures to track Annie. They flew in his helicopter to catch up with the car just in time. Annie was safe!

Annie and Mr. Stacks were together again. They wouldn't let anything keep them apart.

Mr. Stacks decided not to run for mayor after all. Instead, he was going to do something even more important. He was going to adopt Annie. He was going to teach her to read, and take her to movies, and always be there for her.

He was going to be Annie's dad.